SUN FLOWER LION

SUN
FLOWER
LION

KEVIN HENKES

GREENWILLOW BOOKS
An Imprint of HarperCollinsPublishers

Brush and ink were used to prepare the art.

The text type is 22-point ITC Avant Garde Gothic.

Library of Congress Cataloging-in-Publication Data

Names: Henkes, Kevin, author, illustrator.

Title: Sun flower lion / by Kevin Henkes.

Description: First edition. | New York, NY : Greenwillow Books,

an imprint of HarperCollinsPublishers, (2019) |

Summary: Invites the reader to see the sun, bright as a flower,

a flower on a hill that looks like a lion, a lion that dreams

of flowers as big as the sun, and more.

Identifiers: LCCN 2019021131 |

ISBN 9780062866103 (hardback) | ISBN 9780062866110 (lib. bdg.)

Subjects: | CYAC: Lions—Fiction. | Animals—Infancy—Fiction. |

Flowers—Fiction. | Sun—Fiction. | Imagination—Fiction.

Classification: LCC PZ7.H389 Suc 2019 | DDC (E)—dc23

LC record available at https://lccn.loc.gov/2019021131

20 21 22 23 24 WOR 10 9 8 7 6 5 4 3 2 1

First Edition

 GREENWILLOW BOOKS

For Barbara Bader

CHAPTER

1

This is the sun.

Can you see it?

The sun is in the sky.

It is shining.

It is as bright as a flower.

CHAPTER

2

This is a flower.

Can you see it?

The flower is growing.

It is growing on the hill.

It looks like a little lion.

CHAPTER
3

This is a lion.

Can you see him?

The lion is running up the hill.

He smells the flower.

He warms himself in the sun.

CHAPTER

4

The lion sleeps.

He dreams he is in a field of flowers.

The flowers are as big as the sun.

The flowers are cookies.

The lion eats them all.

When he wakes up, he is hungry.

CHAPTER

5

The lion runs home.

Can you see him?

No, you can't.

He is running too fast.

CHAPTER

6

Now the lion is home.

He has had his supper,

and he is asleep with his family.

He is happy.

Can you see him?

Yes, you can.

The End

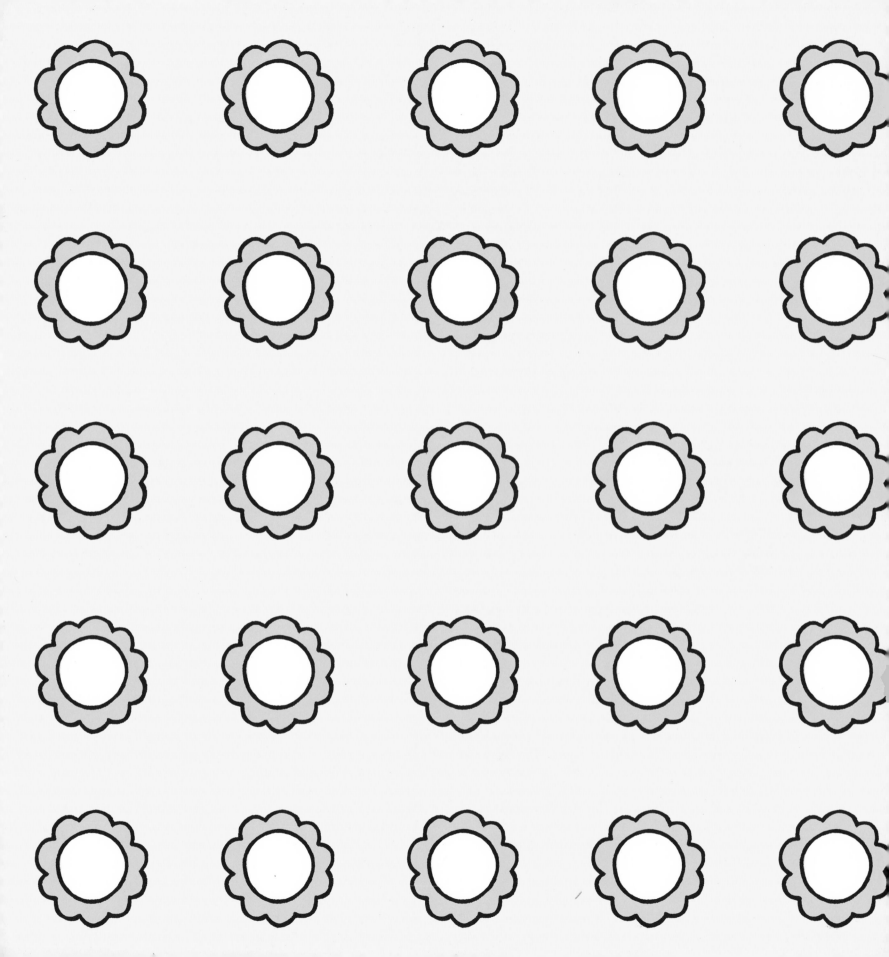